SILLY DILLY DUCK

BY JUNE WOODMAN

ILLUSTRATED BY PAMELA STOREY

BRIMAX BOOKS · NEWMARKET · ENGLAND

Dilly Duck goes to the pond.
Her three little ducklings
go with her.
"Come with me," says Dilly.
"I will take you for a swim
in the duck pond."
But the little ducklings are
afraid. They do not want
to go to the duck pond.
"We do not know how to
swim!" they say.
But Dilly Duck does not
hear them.
Silly Dilly Duck!

Bossy Bear plays with
his roller-skates. He has
a lot of fun.
He sees Dilly Duck come
along the lane. He sees
the three little ducklings
with her.
"Where are you going?"
says Bossy Bear.
"To the duck pond," says the
first little duckling.
"But I do not want to go."

"Why not?" says Bossy Bear.
"I cannot swim," says
the first little duckling.
"We can play a trick," says
Bossy Bear.
"I will go to the duck pond.
You stay here. You can play
with my roller-skates."
The first little duckling
thinks that will be fun.
He puts on the skates.

Dilly Duck is on her way to
have a swim in the duck pond.
The two little ducklings
and Bossy Bear go along too.
But silly Dilly Duck does not
see Bossy Bear.
The two little ducklings and
Bossy Bear think that this
is very funny. Bossy Bear
likes to play funny tricks.

They all go along the lane.
Soon they meet Hoppy Rabbit.
He drives in his little car.
"Where are you going?"
says Hoppy Rabbit.
"To the duck pond," says
the second little duckling.
"But I do not want to go."
"Why not?" says Hoppy.
"I cannot swim," says
the second little duckling.

Hoppy sees Bossy Bear.
"I am a duckling," says Bossy.
Hoppy thinks that this is very
funny.
"I will go to the duck pond
too," he says. "Duckling can
drive my car. This is
a very funny trick. Silly
Dilly Duck cannot see us."
The second little duckling
gets into Hoppy's car.

They all go along the lane.
Dilly Duck,
  Bossy Bear,
    Hoppy Rabbit
and one little duckling.
But Dilly Duck does not see
her very funny ducklings.

Soon they meet Paddy Dog.
Paddy Dog plays with his
little red scooter.
"Where are you going?"
says Paddy Dog.
"To the duck pond," says
the third little duckling.
"But I do not want to go."
"Why not?" says Paddy Dog.
"I cannot swim," says
the third little duckling.

Paddy Dog thinks that
this is very funny.
"Bossy and Hoppy are very
funny ducklings," he says.
"I will play a trick too.
Duckling can play with
my little red scooter.
I will be the third
little duckling. Silly
Dilly Duck will not see."

They all go along the lane.
Dilly Duck,
   Bossy Bear,
      Hoppy Rabbit
         and Paddy Dog.
But no little ducklings!
Ozzie Owl is in the old tree.
"Hoo-hoo-hoo!" he hoots.
Cuddly Cat jumps down from
the tree. She thinks they
are all very funny.

At last they come to the pond.
Flippy Frog and Merry Mole
are there. They say,
"What funny ducklings."
Then Dilly Duck sees them.
She is afraid. She looks all
round for her lost ducklings.
And here they come!
One on skates,
    one in the car,
        one on the scooter.

But the little ducklings go
too fast. They cannot stop!
SPLASH! SPLASH! SPLASH!
Three little ducklings
fall into the pond.
Bossy Bear, Hoppy Rabbit
and Paddy Dog are all afraid.
"What can we do?
The three little ducklings
cannot swim," they say.

"You are silly!" says
Dilly Duck.
"You must know that all little
ducklings can swim."
She hops into the pond too.
Off they go.
Dilly Duck goes first and the
three little ducklings swim
behind her. Silly Dilly Duck
is not so silly after all!

Say these words again

thinks

afraid

first

jumps

duckling

swim

trick

plays

roller-skates

drives

second

funny

scooter

third